TILT

TILT

MARY HOFFMAN

Barrington Stoke

First published in 2017 in Great Britain by
Barrington Stoke Ltd
18 Walker Street, Edinburgh, EH3 7LP

www.barringtonstoke.co.uk

Text © 2017 Mary Hoffman

A CIP catalogue record for this book is available from the British Library upon request

ISBN: 978-1-78112-565-6

Printed in China by Leo

CONTENTS

CHAPTER ONE

Measuring Up

15th March 1298

Today is the big day – Measurement Day!

My father is as nervous as a cat. Never mind that he is Giovanni Pisano, Head Mason of Santa Maria Maggiore as his father was before him. Today he must measure the beautiful, unfinished tower in the presence of two other men and a notary.

I wish I could be there when they take the measurements but I have to stay and help old Marta in the kitchen. We have no idea how long it will take the men to measure the tower, but we have to be ready to feed three hungry extra mouths when they do finish.

You can't see the tower from our kitchen window but you can if you go out of the front door. So I spend the whole morning dashing back and forth between the kitchen and the door, telling Marta I'm just checking how the men are getting on.

No one else is getting any work done. My father's two youngest apprentices, Piero and Antonio, are supposed to be cutting and shaping blocks of marble in the wooden hut they use as a workshop. But they are outside, part of the small crowd watching what's going on at the tower. I spotted them the last time I went to look out of the door of our house.

Antonio waved at me.

"Good morning, Netta!" he called. "Exciting, isn't it?"

Piero shushed him and I could see even at a distance that he was annoyed with his friend for causing heads to turn and people to look towards me.

I was glad they were too far away to expect me to do more than wave back. Some girls might have been flattered by the way these two young men were always paying me attention, but I found it wearisome.

"Netta, Netta! Where are you?" Marta calls.

Marta needs me to help with chopping and peeling, frying and roasting. But what's going on outside is *so* much more interesting than all that. I wish I had a younger sister so I could send her to Marta and I could run out into the breezy sunshine and join the crowd round the tower.

I used to have some older brothers, but they and my mother are dead and I am all the family my father has left. My name is Simonetta, but I'm always called Netta. I'm the last of the great Pisano family of sculptors and stone-carvers. And now I have to go and carve some carrots.

The sun was high in the sky before the men came in for their meal. Antonio and Piero came first, covered in stone dust even though they'd done not a scrap of work all morning. Marta scolded them and sent them off to wash under the pump in our courtyard.

Then came Father, who looked worried. Then the two other men – Signor Guido, son of the late Giovanni di Simone, and Orsello, the Master Joiner. The Notary came with them, but I didn't catch his name. Marta kept me too busy bustling back and forth with bowls of warm scented water and towels before we served the food.

The apprentices didn't say a word. They were usually full of chatter, but today I think they felt a bit alarmed by eating good food at the table with their master, instead of chewing on a bit of bread and cheese in their dusty workshop.

But my father wanted everyone to hear what they had found at the tower, even these two humble stone-cutters. Even me, I think, though he didn't look at me once during the meal.

It was bad news.

I wasn't surprised. I knew exactly why we were having this big measuring day. The tower had a definite tilt from the straight. You could see it with the naked eye. But still I felt so sorry for my father. The thing is, that tower, with its tilt, is a sort of family affair.

Not that our family had anything to do with building it or designing it. The foundations were laid over a hundred years ago. And Father says there is nothing wrong with them. He gets upset when busybodies who know nothing about cutting stone or building towers say the foundations must have been inadequate for the tower to start to lean.

But, as I say, the laying of the foundations was before his time. Before my grandfather's time too. But he was Head Mason here till he died and then my father took over, so he feels we have a family responsibility to put the tilt right.

I know that he wishes I'd been born a boy – or that the four sons he lost had survived. Then we could save the family's reputation as the finest stone masons in Pisa and beyond.

If the tilting tower falls down, Father will feel it as his personal failure.

CHAPTER TWO

A Heavy Responsibility

We haven't always lived here in Pisa, in the shadow of the tilting tower. I was born here sixteen years ago, but we moved to Siena when I was just able to toddle about, because my father was appointed Chief Architect of the black and white cathedral there. So I was brought up in that beautiful walled city. I still miss its buildings of pink stone.

We came back here two years ago when Father was appointed Head Mason of this city of Pisa – and of the tower. "Our" tower, this one that leans, is the bell tower of the glorious cathedral of Santa Maria Maggiore.

Of course I didn't remember the tower from when I was a baby, but I could see as soon as we arrived back in Pisa that something was very wrong.

Only seven floors had been built, but I knew from what my father said that it should have had eight floors. The top one – the one that should hold the bells – wasn't there.

Giovanni di Simone was Head Mason before my father and he had put placements for six bells at the top of the seventh floor of the tower, but as my father told me as we stood gazing up at it, it didn't look right to him.

Or to me.

Oh, I know girls aren't supposed to be interested in the structure of buildings or in stone carving. But all my life I had seen my father come home from his work covered in marble dust or seen him drawing his designs for statues to adorn the front of Siena's cathedral. His work fascinated me, spoke to my every instinct, and I couldn't pretend to be keen on learning how to cook and clean and sew, as real daughters were supposed to.

Maybe if my mother had lived, she might have made me see the point of housework. But she died when I was just a baby in her arms. Old Marta has done her best to be like a mother to me. But I just can't get excited about the chores that fill her days.

It's all so repetitive. You clean a room or a dress and it gets dirty again. You make a huge meal for the family and your visitors and it's gone in minutes. Nothing left but a mess. And then you have to clean the kitchen and scrub the pots and pans. Yawn.

But if you carve a statue or put up a building – yes, even a tower – it's there for ever. Or at least until it topples over in a cloud of dust and broken marble.

I listened to every word of the talk at lunch on Measurement Day, even though everyone there would have said it wasn't meant for me.

"It's clear that the trouble began at the third floor," my father said, when the men were at the stage of eating cheese with last summer's dried figs and drinking wine sweet as honey from our cellar.

Guido looked uncomfortable. His father built those floors. "I don't see how you can tell that," he said.

"I mean no criticism of your father, Signor Guido," my father said. "But some of the columns on the third floor are showing signs of strain and the tower is not yet complete."

Orsello, the Head Joiner, cleared his throat. "I mean no criticism of Guido's father either," he said. "And Guido himself, as soon as he recognised there was a tilt, started building the floors of the tower higher on one side than on the other, to compensate."

Guido sighed and emptied his wine glass. His face was miserable.

I had looked and looked at the tower until I knew every column and every decoration and I knew that it was true that Guido had tried to correct the tilt. From the fourth floor onwards, anyone with a clear eye could see that someone had tried to make the floors of uneven height.

It was mad, of course, because it did nothing to change the stresses or prevent the lean, but it created an illusion that the tower was trying to straighten itself out.

"So what will you do?" the Notary asked. "Stop building? Or demolish the tower before it falls and kills someone?"

Everyone looked towards my father, their faces eager, and I realised what a big decision he had to make.

CHAPTER THREE

Past Triumphs

The meal came to an end and my father chased the apprentices back to their work. They had drunk so much wine at lunch that I didn't think they'd be much use for the rest of the day. Antonio gave me a wink as they left and I glared at him.

My father fell into an armchair and rubbed his hands over his face. I knew he'd been awake since dawn. I left him to doze and went to help Marta clear up. I felt heavy at heart.

When I came back from the kitchen, my father was awake and putting on his cloak to go out.

"Are you going back to work?" I asked.

He shook his head. "Just out for a walk."

"Can I come with you?"

It was a fine day, but not yet summer and there was a chill in the air. I pulled my shawl around me as I drank in great gulps of fresh air. It was good to be out of the house.

"That was a fine meal you made," Father said. "It was a difficult day and yet there were no voices or fists raised."

It was natural for our footsteps to take us to the tower. In spite of its tilt, it was so beautiful. My father even patted one of the columns on the ground floor as we walked around it, as if it was a favourite horse.

As always I counted the columns.

"Fifteen," my father muttered.

"I know," I whispered.

He stopped in surprise. "You know there are fifteen columns on this floor?"

"Yes, and thirty on each of the other floors," I said.

"How?"

"I looked," I said. "And I can count."

"But why?" he asked. "I didn't think you'd be interested."

"Father, I might be a girl, but I care about the tower as much as you do."

"You do?"

I almost laughed at the puzzled look on his face. "First Grandfather and now you are in charge of this tower. You want to put right what Guido and his father got wrong."

"You understand," he said.

"Of course!" I said. "And you wish you had a son to help you finish it, instead of a daughter and some useless apprentices."

He took my hand. "Ah, but if I had lost you as well as my sons ... then I wouldn't have this face to remind me of your mother."

I was glad of the love in his voice, but I noticed how he hadn't denied he would like a son too, to carry on our family trade.

Our steps turned towards the great cathedral and we walked beyond it to the Baptistery. Looking at it always seemed to soothe my father.

"I was just a child, younger than you are now, when your grandfather finished the dome," he said.

"And he made the pulpit inside too, didn't he?"

I knew this of course, but I wanted him to think about our family's triumphs, not disasters that might be coming our way.

"He did," my father said. "It is his masterpiece."

"And you carved the statues at the top, didn't you?" I asked him.

"I did," he said and I could tell from his face that he was thinking back to those days before he went to Siena to help his father work on the pulpit in the cathedral there.

"You see," I said. "You've done so much fine work. You will solve the problem of the tower, I'm sure."

He squeezed my hand and I was glad I had cheered him up. That was something I could do, at least.

CHAPTER FOUR

Spring Onions

Something changed after that day. My father started to talk to me about his work. Not much to start with but, as soon as he discovered how much I already knew and how keen I was, he took me more and more into his confidence.

I still had to darn holes in the bed linen while we talked. And I still had all the same chores in the house. But now I had something more interesting to think about than the best way to get stains out of a table cloth.

I had found a way to deal with the apprentices too. Antonio was always bolder than Piero, but they both made cow's eyes at me whenever they saw me.

The apprentices took their midday meal in the workshop, but they always ate their supper with us in the house and they slept in a lean-to out in our courtyard. You had to cross the yard to get to the privy and the washing line was out there. I couldn't avoid meeting the young men several times a day.

But I could divert them. So I started asking them about their work too.

At first they were puzzled. No one had ever taken an interest in what they did all day before – not even their own mothers!

"Well, we just dress the stone," Piero said.

"But your father is going to teach us how to carve it into statues," said Antonio.

I knew my father had trained many apprentices in his time and some of them went on to become fine, well-known artists in their own right. Perhaps these two cow-eyed apprentices would also have successful lives as sculptors or builders one day?

I encouraged them to tell me more. And it turned out they weren't just dressing stone, making it smooth to use for building. They were learning a lot about the different properties of marble and how best to handle it.

"You can't just cut it out of the mountain side and start using it straight away," Piero told me.

"No," said Antonio, who was eager to show off his knowledge. "You have to let it lie for at least a year."

"What does that do?" I asked.

Antonio scratched his head. "Well, if there are any flaws, they sort of come out by the end of the year. Then, if the marble hasn't shown anything bad, you can start dressing and carving."

This was news to me. I knew you had to let wood season after the trees had been cut down and before you used it for buildings or for furniture, but I had no idea marble could be the same.

"Have you ever been to a marble quarry?" I asked the apprentices, but they shook their heads. I decided to ask my father about it the first chance I had.

The next day at midday I went out to the vegetable patch and dug up some of the first onions of spring – the tender ones with small white bulbs and long green leaves. I washed them in the kitchen sink, shook off the water and took them to the workshop.

"Hello," I called from the door. "I've come with something to liven up your bread and cheese."

Of course it was just an excuse to see inside the workshop and spy on what they were doing, but the apprentices were delighted to add the fresh onions to their lunch.

They went on with their meal while I wandered round the shed, looking at tools and blocks of marble and asking questions.

The two apprentices hadn't moved past the simple mallets and chisels used for shaping and dressing the raw stone into blocks, but I wanted to know what all the tools were for.

Piero and Antonio came over and showed me the more advanced tools. These were used by senior pupils and by my father himself – the chisels graded from a heavy tool for carving the rough shapes down to a much smaller one for fine details.

"I did this," Antonio said, showing me some rough blobby bits of stone with pride.

"Mm," I said. "Lovely."

"It's acanthus leaves," Piero said helpfully. "They go at the top of pillars."

"Of course one of the senior apprentices will work on them to shape them more into leaves," Antonio admitted. "But I'm allowed to do the first bit."

"I'm sure it won't be long before you progress to the leaves," I said, though I had my doubts.

Ever since I became aware of the world around me, I had seen the complex statues and decorations my father had created from marble. But this was the first time I really appreciated how skilled he was. He could take these shapeless lumps of stone and transform them into leaves without even thinking about it.

An acanthus leaf was one thing. But a tower that rose straight and true into the sky quite another. And what I wanted to know was how you got from the leaf to the tower.

CHAPTER FIVE

Buildings in the Mind

I found myself thinking about the tower all the time. I didn't want to be a stone-cutter like the apprentices or a master sculptor like my father. This was just as well, since I had never heard of any women working in those arts. And it's true that the stone-cutters and sculptors needed more strength than I had in my arms. But I had seen women down at the harbour haul in nets full of fish, and their shoulders were as broad and strong as those of our apprentices.

Building a tower was brain work, at least at the beginning. True, you needed stone-cutters to shape the blocks and carve the columns, but all of that was useless unless you first had a plan – an idea of what was to be built and how.

I found a piece of charcoal in my father's workshop and I tried to draw our tower on the white wall of the scullery. I failed miserably. It was like a child's drawing of a building, too fuzzy and not at all accurate. No one could build a tower from scratch based on my drawing.

And then, as I stood there sadly, Marta bustled in to scold me for "making a mess" on her "nice clean scullery wall"!

That night the apprentices took their candles and went yawning to their beds straight after supper. There was nothing like a day of working stone to make them sleep like babies. I asked my father who had first designed the tower.

"He was called Diotisalvi," he said.

"*God Save You*," I said. "How did he get such a funny name?"

"Maybe because that's how he greeted everyone," my father said. "Anyway, he was the same man who planned out the Baptistery."

"How did anyone know what to do?" I asked as I threaded my needle. "I mean, how did the idea get from God Save You's head to the hands of the men who were to build the tower?"

"Oh, old God Save You had the plan laid out clear in his head," my father said. "All the measurements and dimensions. And he would have made notes – how tall, how wide, the size and depth of the foundations. But those notes haven't survived. He started the Baptistery nearly a hundred and fifty years ago."

"And then Grandfather and you finished it off?"

"Yes, but a hundred years passed from its first foundation stone to when my father took it over. And that was about twenty years after the Baptistery." My father looked at me. "Why do you want to know all this?"

"I'm interested," I said. "All the buildings here in the piazza have been our family's life and work – since long before I was born."

All of a sudden I felt weary at the thought. All this talk of hundreds of years when I had only lived for sixteen on this earth! And my father was nearly fifty. How could I hope to understand a fraction of what he knew?

I took him out to the scullery and showed him my drawing. I blushed and felt shy. It looked even more like a child's scribble than ever.

My father didn't agree. "This is a beautiful portrait of the bell tower," he said. "You have shown as many columns as you could from one angle and the number of floors and terraces is quite right."

"But I drew what I saw," I said. "I want to know how to draw what isn't there yet."

"To draw what isn't there yet?" he said.

"Yes, to make a drawing of a building *before* it's been built," I insisted.

"You mean a plan, Netta? Something to show the stone cutters and masons?"

"Yes, exactly. How can I show *all* the columns and the foundations, too, which you can't see because they're underground?"

I was fizzing with ideas. How could I have lived all my life as the daughter of such a great architect and sculptor and never thought about any of these questions before?

My father got up and paced around the room. "Your drawing is a work of art," he said. "But what you are talking about now is a work of precise calculation and measurement. It is more like mathematics."

My excitement went flat and my heart sank. No one would teach mathematics to a girl like me. Unless ... "Father, can you teach me?" I asked.

"Teach you mathematics?"

"Yes," I begged. "Teach me what I need to understand to design a building and to put that design down so someone else might build the building I see in my mind."

"Such a thing has never been done!" Father said, and his voice was loud with shock.

"You mean no woman has ever done it," I said. I was close to tears, but it was vital he shouldn't think me a silly girl, not now. "Would you have taught me if I had been your son?" I asked.

Father was silent for a long time. "What will happen to you if you do this?" he said at last.

"What do you mean?"

"I want you to lead the life of a normal woman," he said. "To marry and have children, my grandchildren."

I kept my voice steady. "You mean grand*sons*, don't you? A new generation of boys who could learn your skills. But what if I marry and give birth to ten girls? Or I die in childbirth, like my mother –?"

I stopped as my father sat down and put his face in his hands. I had gone too far.

"I'm sorry, Father," I said. "I didn't mean to stir up old grief. I miss her too."

"You are right," he said. "A woman's life is full of dangers. But so is a Head Mason's. I might fall from that cursed tower to my death. Or be crushed under it if it falls on me. There are many ways in which that tower could be the death of me."

"And if that should happen – which I pray to God it won't – all your knowledge and skill would be buried in your tomb with you," I said. I struggled to keep my voice steady and low.

"I have my pupils and apprentices," my father said, but I could hear the doubt in his voice.

CHAPTER SIX

Everything Changes

The very next day my father surprised me by coming home at midday with a young woman. She was a healthy-looking, big-boned girl and for one wild moment I thought she was going to be his new bride, a woman to bear him more sons to follow him in his work.

We all stood in silence until at last my father said, "This is Pina."

She bobbed a shy curtsey to me. "Good day, Signorina," she said.

"Good day," I said, and I looked towards my father.

"Pina is coming to live with us," he told me. "Marta is no longer young and the chores are too much for you alone. You can show Pina what's needed and in a few weeks you will have more time."

"More time for what?" I asked.

My father smiled. "To help me with my work," he said. "If you wish."

If I wished ...

I almost danced for joy I was so thrilled!

But Marta was outraged when I took Pina to the kitchen. Not because she was getting another pair of hands to help with all the work about the house. She was very pleased about that. But I was foolish and I told her why my father had brought this new addition into our household.

"Help him with his work?" Marta said. "In what way? Who will marry a girl who hauls blocks of marble up the tower with the apprentice boys?" She looked at me in horror. "Whatever next?"

I didn't say anything, but I bristled inside. She shouldn't have spoken to me like that. But I bit my tongue, because Marta had looked after me since I was a baby and she was more like an aunt than a servant.

My head was in a whirl. Did my father really mean to teach me his skills? Would I be able to learn them? And how long would Pina take to learn *her* chores so that I would have the free time he promised?

Come to that, where was this new member of the household going to sleep? I groaned. My father's kindness had given me a new problem. I left Pina chopping herbs in the kitchen with Marta while I went to sweep out an attic room and lay down a fresh straw mattress for her.

Pina was a capable, strong young woman and a quick learner, but still it took a full three weeks before I could leave her to work with Marta. There was a lot for her to learn. And I had to teach her how to avoid the apprentices too, as they seemed happy to switch their interest from me to her. I didn't mind. I had been trying to put them off for so long that it was no shock when they turned their eyes to the next young female who came along.

So, we were well into April and the spring was lovely. There were blue skies over Pisa and the air felt soft and full of possibilities. I had never felt so alive as I did the first morning my father took me out to the tower. This was no family stroll round the piazza, but a serious matter. I could no longer complain that I didn't know anything about my father's work – he was going to explain everything in the greatest possible detail.

"Every building begins with the foundations," he told me.

"What about the design?" I asked. "The idea for the building."

He sighed. "I told you. I think God Save You had the final design worked out before the tower's foundations were laid. But for all those who worked on the tower it was enough that it was going be circular and have these dimensions. The rest – all the columns along the terraces and the decoration – would come later as the men worked on it."

"So, tell me the dimensions," I replied.

"The base is fifty feet measured all round. The walls are thirteen feet thick and the foundations have the same thickness."

"How deep are the foundations?" I asked, as my mind worked out what I needed to know.

"Nearly ten feet," my father said. "And those ten feet should have been enough."

He unlocked the great wooden door of the tower and led me inside. There was no one but us, since work had halted while the tilt was measured and new plans were made. I stood looking up at the blue sky that showed through the top of the tower. It was hollow in the middle, like a tube of cool marble.

"The foundations support the perimeter walls," my father said. "Here in the middle there are no foundations."

"Why is there nothing in the middle?" I asked. I had never thought about any of this before. "And no floors above us on any of the levels. Wouldn't that strengthen the tower?"

My father laughed. "You are already thinking like a builder," he said. "The hole in the middle is because of earthquakes. If it wasn't hollow and there had been an earthquake like the one twenty years before the foundations were laid, the tower would have fallen."

I had never experienced an earthquake, but then I had lived so few years compared with how long this tower had stood on the earth. I tried to imagine what an earthquake would feel like to someone standing inside the tower. But my father was still talking.

"It is normal to leave foundations to settle for at least a year," he said. "That's what was done here and after a year it seemed safe to build."

I looked round at the thick walls, then touched their cool, dense surface. "So," I asked, "why did it start to lean?"

CHAPTER SEVEN

The Staircase

"Come," my father said. "I'll show you why. Let's go up the stairs."

I hadn't noticed the stairs before but I was eager to climb up to the next floor, where I'd be able to look out between the columns.

The staircase was a wide spiral of marble, with steps winding upwards, floor by floor, between the inner and outer walls. The spiral soon brought us out at the second level. We stepped out on to the terrace and walked around the whole of the tower, looking out between the columns.

It made me feel quite dizzy. I looked down at our house and I could see Pina hanging out bed linen in the courtyard.

A bit further off was the large shed where my father's apprentices worked. And in the other direction was the Cathedral and the Baptistery beyond it. I could see details on the cathedral I had never noticed from ground level. At the east end was a half circle like a tower sliced down the middle, which had the same sort of narrow columns as we were standing between now.

"See those?" my father asked. "Those columns were added by God Save You. By the time he came to think of this tower, he wanted to make a whole column of columns – he thought they were architecture at its most elegant."

I looked at the columns and they gave me a strange feeling now that I was actually on the tower. It was obvious that it was leaning by at least a few feet, but its tilt made the columns on the cathedral opposite us look as if *they* were out of true. But that was the reverse of the truth. I trembled, wondering what it would be like if the tower were to collapse at this very moment, with just me and my father on it.

But I also felt wonderfully free. It was not often that I got out of the house or spent time alone with my father. Now my mind was empty of thoughts of steaming cabbage or bleaching linen, it was open to all the new sensations rushing in. I was high up above my usual life, looking at the world with fresh eyes. My mind was full, buzzing as questions and new ideas jostled each other.

"Can you see any reason for the tilt?" my father asked.

I took my time before replying. After all, this was the question that all the local builders and masons had been struggling to answer for years!

I walked around the terrace again, looking carefully at every column and block of stone. They all seemed to be well made, with perfect proportions and a beautiful sense of scale.

I wanted so much to say something intelligent, something to make my father proud, to show him I understood. I remembered he had said on Measurement Day that the trouble began at the third level.

"Can we go up one more floor?" I asked.

"Of course. We can go to the top. You are right to want to see it all first, before you answer my question."

We began again to climb up the marble staircase. I was glad that there were walls on both sides so that I couldn't see how high up I now was. We walked around the terrace of the third level and I saw the cracks and splits in the stone that Father had mentioned. But I couldn't see any reason for the breaks. The blocks and columns looked as well made as those on the floors below.

But on the fourth floor all the columns looked in poor shape.

At last we stood in the belfry at the top of the seventh level. The view from up here made me feel like an eagle soaring over the cathedral square.

But still I had seen nothing that could account for the tilt.

We walked back down the steps in silence. I counted nearly 300. Only when we were out on the grass surrounding the tower and my father was locking the wooden door did he speak again.

"Well, Netta?" he said. "Tell me your ideas."

The sunlight dazzled me and I felt as if I had been holding my breath.

"I am sure of nothing, Father," I said. "The foundations, you assure me, are sound. The round shape is one that should be stable. I can think of only two explanations."

"Tell me."

"Either there is a fault in the ground under the tower or some faulty materials have been used somewhere – but I'm sure I couldn't see any."

He came closer and clasped my arms. I think if I had been a boy he would have clapped me on the back.

"You have hit on two main causes!" he said. "But there is a third and today we have walked up and down it."

"The staircase!"

But what could be wrong with that strong marble spiral? Then we both said it at once.

"It's too heavy!"

CHAPTER EIGHT

Causes

We stared at each other and I could see the twinkle in my father's eyes. I couldn't help but grin back at him and I felt very pleased with myself.

Our footsteps were taking us back along the south wall of the cathedral to the Baptistery, where I had been given my name sixteen years before.

"All this part of Pisa used to be a lagoon," my father said. "The ground under our feet was once water."

"When?" I asked, and I imagined wading and splashing across the piazza.

"Hundreds of years ago," he told me. "In the end it got silted up with all the soil that was washed down the River Arno."

"But why didn't it just end up in the sea?" I asked.

"The force of the waves pushing into the mouth of the river was so great that it prevented the soil from escaping," Father said. "So over the course of hundreds of years, the lagoon filled up and became ground firm enough to build on."

He stopped walking and waved his arms at the grassy land around us.

"Just imagine," he said. "First a lagoon where ships could enter from the sea and sail up the river. Then bit by bit the lagoon fills up with sludge and the ships can't navigate it. At last it becomes land and all these marvellous buildings are created!"

It made me feel very peculiar to think we were now standing on what used to be a lagoon full of ships, with salt water flowing in from the sea and fresh water flowing out from the river. But in the end the land had won.

"Is this land still wet?" I asked, as all of a sudden I thought I understood. "I mean, is there still water in the earth?"

"Yes. It makes the ground much softer than anywhere else in the city."

"So if the ground is soft that softness could cause the buildings to sink – or to lean?"

My father nodded, his face grave.

"Then why aren't they all sinking?" I asked, panic in my voice as I had a sudden vision of all the beautiful monuments wallowing into the ground. It made everything seem unsafe, as if everything I had believed about my life so far had been based on an untruth. I swear I felt the ground give way beneath me.

"Remember it was hundreds of years ago that the lagoon was here," my father said, and he took hold of my arm. "Much of the ground has dried out and is quite firm. But parts are unpredictable. Perhaps the ground under the south side of the tower has more water in it and that's why the tower is sinking there."

I thought that my father could be right, but then I remembered something else.

"What about the materials?" I asked. "The marble all looks good to me."

"Well, just as foundations have to be left to settle for a year before you build – it's the same with marble."

"You have to leave it for a year?" I asked, and then I remembered what Piero the apprentice had told me.

"Yes. The marble has been dug out of the mountains where it has lain in the dark and the damp. It needs to breathe in the air and feel both sunlight and frost on it before it gives up its secrets."

"Secrets?" I said.

"Yes. Flaws or cracks or changes in colour might emerge in that year. If they do, then the stone masons know what marble to discard and what marble is safe to use."

"But we do that here, don't we?" I said. "I've seen the shed where the marble is left to rest."

My father nodded. "Yes, but when the fourth level of the tower was being built the marble was used too soon, before it had a year to prove itself sound."

I knew enough now about the tower's history to guess whose fault that had been. "That was in Guido's father's time?"

He waited a while before replying, as if this was a truth he was not keen to speak. "It was Giovanni di Simone who took over the building from the fourth level," he said at last. "He was the Head Mason then. But we shouldn't be too fast to judge and blame him. Perhaps the Clerk of the Works or others above him told him to hurry up and get on with the building. Perhaps he was under terrible pressure to use the marble on the inner walls before it was ready."

I could see that my father didn't want to think badly of someone who had been Head Mason before him.

"Well, now we have soft ground and bad marble," I said. I counted those flaws off on my fingers and marvelled that the tower had stayed up this long. "Next – the staircase ..."

My father sighed. "We'd better walk back home," he said. "We can talk about the staircase later."

CHAPTER NINE

An Unexpected Visitor

But when we got home a visitor was waiting for us.

Marta was in a terrible state. She had been forced to entertain this young man on her own, since she didn't think it was right for Pina to wait on him. Instead she had sent Pina out to wave up at us on the tower. But we had been too deep in conversation to see or hear her.

"Filippo!" my father said, taking the young man's hand. "How are you? And how is your father?"

They were chatting away like old friends before my father remembered I was there.

"Filippo, this is my daughter, Simonetta," he said. "Netta, we call her."

Filippo made a neat little bow and took my hand. He was a nice-looking boy, perhaps a couple of years older than me, with dark eyes and a mop of curly black hair.

"I know Filippo's family from our time in Siena," my father explained. "His father, Tommaso, was one of the cathedral masons."

Marta seemed relieved that she no longer had to make small talk with this unexpected visitor. She bustled away to the kitchen and was soon laying the table with a meal for us all.

As we ate, I puzzled about Filippo. He seemed very pleasant and his manners were good. I had no memory of meeting any of his family in Siena, but I enjoyed hearing news from there. But why was he here? Perhaps he wanted a job at Santa Maria Maggiore if he was a mason like his father. Or perhaps he wanted to become my father's apprentice.

I was disappointed when the two men went out to walk round the cathedral piazza without me. Was Father going to talk to this interloper about the defects in the tower? Now that he had taken me into his confidence at last I didn't like that idea.

I could get nothing out of Marta about Filippo, and I understood why she hadn't left our new maid with him when a blushing Pina declared him "very handsome".

Marta did tell me that my father had asked for a room to be made ready for Filippo – as he would be staying for "a few days". So, while Marta and Pina cleared the table of our meal, I had to put the tower out of my head and sweep, clean and fold linen – all the tasks I had done before Pina joined us. By the time the two men came back I was in a dark mood, but I had to smile and be polite to our guest.

At last, as we ate our evening meal together and drank my father's good red wine, I began to relax in Filippo's company. He was friendly and his nice manners calmed my rather hostile mood. And he included me in his conversation with my father about the buildings of Pisa that were as familiar to me as my own hands.

"You are so lucky to live here close to the cathedral square," he said to me, over a dish of grapes and walnuts. "The buildings are all so elegant, so beautiful."

Well, of course I agreed with that! Hadn't my father and grandfather between them had a hand in all of them?

"Even the bell tower," Filippo added.

"In some ways the most beautiful," I said, boldly. "For me, its imperfection adds to its character."

He nodded and I felt a surge of friendship for him. But nothing in our conversation that evening hinted at why he had visited us.

Next morning Filippo went off with my father to inspect the works while I was left behind with nothing much to do. So I went out for a walk by myself.

My footsteps took me back to the tower where my father had come close to telling me about the third cause of its tilt. We had agreed the marble staircase was too heavy, but was that all there was to it? Would that be enough to tip the whole tower out of true?

The longer I looked at the bell tower, the more I realised all the things I didn't know. However much I tried to think like a builder and designer there

45

was so much more knowledge I needed if I were to help my father solve the problem.

So by the time Father and Filippo came back for the midday meal my mood was dark again, this time with sadness and frustration. It was a chilly day for April and I was glad that Marta had made a hearty soup.

As we dipped our chunks of bread into the soup, I was aware of Filippo giving me looks full of meaning, but I had no idea what that meaning might be. After Marta cleared his bowl, he went out alone and my father said he needed to talk to me in private.

My father cleared his throat and said, "Filippo would like to marry you."

"What?" I almost choked. "But he only met me for the first time yesterday!"

"Nevertheless ..." my father said. "Filippo has come to Pisa with the purpose of seeking a wife."

He held up his hand to stop me speaking.

"Don't answer now," he said. "You must think about it. Filippo is the son of one of my dearest friends. He is of an age to marry. He works with his father and is a steady, sober sort of fellow. He wants a wife who understands that work and he knew that I had a daughter of an age to marry. So he came here to ask you."

"Then why didn't he?" I demanded, and a hot rage grew inside me. "Why did he ask you to do it instead? Was it because he knew I would laugh in his face? What kind of man marries someone they haven't spoken two words to?" I glared across the table at my father. "Was that how you courted my mother?"

My father put his head in his hands.

CHAPTER TEN

Parting

I had to stoke my anger or I would have burned with embarrassment. When Filippo got in, I came straight to the point.

"My father has conveyed your kind offer to me," I said with an icy manner that hid my real feelings. "I am, of course, flattered but I'm afraid my answer must be no."

He looked wretched. "May I ask why?" he said. "Do I displease you?"

"You neither displease nor please me," I said. "I don't know you. I have only just met you. But I have no wish to marry anyone. I am content to stay here with my father. Did you imagine we'd live in Siena?"

He spread his hands. "It is where I was born. Where my family live."

"Well, my family live in Pisa," I said. "And here I will stay. This is my city, as Siena is yours, and I have a life that keeps me here."

I was so bold that I thought he would accept my answer, but he wasn't giving up.

"And yet you lived in my city for some years," he said. "It would not be unfamiliar to you."

"*You* would be unfamiliar to me," I snapped. "I met you only yesterday and you have already made a sort of business proposition to my father. You can't claim to have any feelings for me."

"I feel great respect," he said. "Your father has told me of the interest you take in his work and of your quick wits. I admire you. And I believe I could love you. You are very beautiful after all."

His words took me by surprise and now I was blushing like a foolish girl, redder even than Pina. No one had ever told me I was beautiful. And right after telling me I was clever!

"Thank you," I said. "I ... I am not refusing you because I don't like you."

"But you are refusing me."

"Yes. Because I don't know you. And because I don't want to marry anyone."

"It has been too sudden," he said. "I should have waited."

And now he looked sad, like a man rejected by the woman he truly loved. I felt a wild urge to laugh but I didn't want to hurt his feelings. Even though I didn't believe he had any strong feelings for me. How could he have?

"Are there no suitable young women in Siena?" I asked instead. "I am sure you would have more success if you asked one of them."

"So your answer is really no?" he asked, and he reached towards me as if he would like to take my hand.

"I'm afraid so," I said, and I put both hands behind my back. "I wish you well, but marriage is not for me. I have other plans for my life."

"You want to become a nun?" he asked, with a puzzled look on his face.

I wondered what he would say if I told him I wanted to learn mathematics, understand the mysteries of marble, design buildings. But instead I shook my head.

"Then there is no more to be said," he said. "I will find your father and make my farewells."

"You are leaving today?"

"There is no reason to stay," he said.

And now I felt sad that Filippo was going. We didn't often have visitors and it had made a change to have someone new in the house. But I understood why he wouldn't want to stay. Filippo might not have had any deep feelings for me, but I had hurt his pride.

"Oh, I'm sorry he's gone," Pina said at breakfast the next day. "He was so handsome and what lovely manners ...!"

That made me grumpy for the rest of the week. Even my father seemed a little afraid of me. I didn't mind – my anger made me feel powerful.

But when I had calmed down, I put Filippo and his unexpected offer right out of my head. It was true what I had told him. I didn't want to get married – at least not for a very long time.

I wanted to find out more about the structure and design of buildings and how to make them strong and keep them standing even on land that had once been water. I wanted to learn everything my father could teach me about that world and, if I could, to be part of it myself.

But, to tell the truth, I was afraid of marriage. Or rather, I was afraid of having babies, which was what usually followed fast on the heels of a wedding. My mother wasn't the only woman who had lost her life giving birth to another.

I would have to have very strong feelings indeed for a man before I risked my life to make children with him. And I didn't have those feelings for Filippo or for any man I had yet seen.

CHAPTER ELEVEN

Back up the Staircase

It took a while for us to settle down after Filippo's visit. Somehow, Pina and Marta both knew he had asked me to marry him and that I had refused him. I didn't tell them and I'm sure my father wouldn't have, but I don't think I imagined their looks of pity.

But, then, I asked my father to take me up the tower again. I wanted him to understand that I was serious about what I wanted to learn. This time we didn't go far up because I stopped him as we stood on the stairs.

"Tell me about the staircase," I said.

"Think of it," he said, and he pointed to the wide steps. "I've heard stories that you could ride a horse up here!"

I could just imagine it. A rider on a white horse. And he had the face of Filippo. I waved my hand in front of my face to banish the image. It must have looked as if I was swatting a fly away.

"Do you think anyone ever did?" I asked.

My father shrugged. "It could be done – if you had a very well-trained horse. But the real trouble is the weight."

He spread his arms to touch both walls of the staircase.

"The tower is really two towers, one inside the other. And the staircase is contained in the outside and inside cylinders. As you see, it is made of marble. Why do you think the tower needed a staircase at all?"

"Why, to reach the bells to ring them."

"That's one reason. But you could have built a wooden ramp for that, as is normal in other bell towers. After all, the bell ringers are just another kind of workman. They don't need anything so grand as marble."

I was beginning to understand.

"The design of this tower," he went on, "was unusual in every way. The idea of the open terraces, with all the columns, was that fine gentlemen and ladies, nobles from this city and beyond, could go up the tower for a wonderful view of any festival or procession going on below."

"And they couldn't walk up a ramp?" I asked.

Father shook his head. "It had to be as grand a staircase as they could afford to build. And that meant marble."

"So the nobles and visitors had to be able to reach any of the outside galleries? And the stairs had to reach to the top?" I wanted to be sure I understood.

"That's right," my father said. "And this changed all the usual rules for designing bell towers. Usually, you start with a solid base and, as you build upwards, the walls get thinner. You start with a window with a single arch, then on the higher levels, the windows have two arches or three, up to five arches to a window."

I couldn't make sense of this. "But why?" I asked.

"To make the tower lighter and more flexible towards the top," my father said. "Then, when the bells ring, the power of the vibrations doesn't bring down the whole structure."

I hadn't thought about that. Pisa was full of towers – some were private ones built as defences, others were bell towers for our many churches. When all the bells of our city rang out at once, you could feel the very air vibrate.

"So," I said, and I looked at my father. "If you had designed this tower, that's how you would have done it?"

"I think so," he said. "The point is that this internal staircase meant it wasn't possible to put in those windows. And it added so much extra weight to the walls."

"No wonder the tower began to sink!" I said.

"That and the softer ground to the south," my father agreed. "And building with marble that hadn't been left to stand for a year."

I nodded. At last I felt I understood so much more than I had.

"Let's climb up to the fourth floor," Father said, and he led the way.

Father was out of breath by the time we got there. I looked at him properly, as I hadn't done for a long time. His body seemed as strong and wiry as ever – his work kept him as fit as a much younger man. But I saw the grey in his hair and how thin it was. His scalp was showing in places.

I felt a terrible, tender pang. One day my father was going to die and leave me. I couldn't bear the thought and I thrust it to the back of my mind. What I had to do was relieve him of the pressure in his life. I must act like a lacework of windows and take some of the stress away from this man who was the solid foundation of my life.

Together we stepped out on to the gallery of the fourth floor.

It was wonderful to leave the confined space of the two walls and stand out in the fresh air between the columns. From the ground the columns looked slender and elegant but up close they were solid and reassuring.

My father walked round to the north side. "Tell me what's different here from on the other side," he said.

I took my time. I walked the whole circuit of the fourth floor terrace more than once. I had no tools to measure with, but I thought I could see a difference.

"The south side is higher," I said.

"Yes, it is. It's six and a half inches higher on the south than on the north."

"Who did that?"

"Guido's father, Giovanni di Simone. He thought he could correct the problem by making the galleries higher on the south side – and so sort of straighten it up."

"But his idea didn't work?"

"As you see," my father said, and he waved his hand to take in the whole structure, "there's been no building work done here for twenty years! Since before you were born. And it falls to me to sort out what to do next."

CHAPTER TWELVE
The Belfry

For a moment I was infected by my father's despair.
The task was huge and what could I do in the face
of such an enormous duty? Even my gifted, clever
and hard-working father was at a loss. He had
years of experience – it was an impertinence for a
young girl like me to imagine she might help.

My father was already walking up the staircase
to the next floor and I had to follow. That was
the secret. You had to keep on walking, thinking,
trying. I followed him up as fast as I could, but
he seemed to have regained his energy and was
taking the stairs easily. We didn't stop at the fifth
or sixth floors but kept going until we reached the
seventh and final floor.

"Old Giovanni kept on building the floors a bit higher on the south side," Father said, no longer out of breath. "The fifth, sixth and seventh floors aren't even. And he made other changes. You can see the decorations and sculptures are much simpler, less ornate than elsewhere. He just wanted to press on and make a building that could be used."

"And the decoration can't be seen from the ground," I said.

"Nor will the nobles come up as high as this ..."

"Because only the bell ringers would be allowed in the belfry ..."

My father frowned. "Giovanni made it the belfry, but it's not right," he said. "There should be an eighth floor with the bells."

"But this one has been made to hold bells," I pointed out.

"Only six," Father replied, and his voice was sharp. "It should have twelve bells, to ring out the most divine combination of notes."

I looked around me. There were indeed six arches for bells on this seventh floor, but no bells hung there. Our tower could make no music as it was.

"The tower should be a hundred *braccia* tall, according to my calculations," Father said. "Without the eighth floor, which I believe God Save You meant to be added, it won't reach that."

"So, will you add the eighth floor?" I asked, but then a horrible vision struck me. My father would build another floor and then the whole tower would topple over, like a child's pile of bricks when she adds the top one.

"I haven't decided," he said, and I could tell he shared that fear too. "The tower now tilts by two and a half feet. I have to calculate whether to risk building higher."

We came down the staircase slowly – we both had a lot to think about.

When we reached the bottom I turned and spoke to my father. "How can I help?" I asked.

"You know," he said, "it helps me to talk to you about it. I can't show my fears and doubts to the pupils and apprentices. They have to have complete faith in my knowledge and skill."

"I'm proud you are willing to talk to me about it, Papa," I said, my heart full. "But I don't know enough to be able to make useful suggestions. That's why I want you to teach me everything you know."

"And you'd really rather do that than marry Filippo and raise a family?" my father asked.

"Really I would!" I cried. "Besides, I want to stay here in Pisa with you – not live in Siena."

"Then we must make the most of you," he said, and he put his arm round me. "You were right when we talked before. I had been thinking only of passing my skills on to a son and when your brothers' lives were cut short and I lost your mother too, I despaired. But you, my daughter, have given me hope."

From then on, Father and I could be found every evening studying drawings on parchment until our tallow candles guttered out. Marta tut-tutted about the number of candles we used, especially after the summer had come and gone and the nights drew in.

My father was much better at drawing than I was, but by watching and copying him, I was improving.

Parchment was precious and when he had finished with a drawing he scraped it clean so that we could use it again. His drawings were always marked with notes and numbers. Mine were less business-like and more artistic. But, as we talked and drew, I began to understand more about weight and stress and the strength of different shapes.

We talked late into every night about how the tower could gain its eighth floor and its proper belfry without causing it to lean further out of the true.

"We must build it up to the full hundred *braccia*," my father would say. "It's not only what God Save You had in mind in his original plan, but it will then – as is proper – match the height of the Cathedral and the Baptistery."

I loved the fact that he now said "we" when he talked. We both became obsessed by the idea of the belfry and soon believed that it was up to us to build the eighth floor and finish the tower as it had been designed over a hundred years before.

CHAPTER THIRTEEN

Christmas in Pisa

The year turned and we were heading to the low point of winter and we still had not come to any final decision about how to realise our dream.

On the 6th of December a parcel came for me from Siena – the first I had ever had in my life. I unwrapped it to find a fine red woollen shawl – sent by Filippo. I was astonished to realise that he still thought of me and ashamed that I had sent no Saint Nicholas Day gift to him. But it had never occurred to me. I had assumed I would never see him again.

I wrapped the shawl around me and its warmth and softness felt like an embrace. I couldn't help but think of what my Christmas would be like had I accepted Filippo's proposal, but I shook the idea out of my head. There was no way I could have left my father – or the tower. But I still wore Filippo's red shawl, despite Marta and Pina's strange looks.

In those weeks I went back to helping Marta in the kitchen. We always put on a grand feast on Christmas Eve for all the apprentices and the men who worked under my father. With all the plucking and roasting and pie-making that needed to be done, I couldn't be spared for building matters.

I learned that Guido was coming to the feast. I hadn't seen him since Measurement Day and I was uneasy about meeting him again. His father had done his best to correct the tilt in the tower, but it seemed he had also agreed to use poor quality marble on the fourth floor. I had to keep telling myself that none of this was Guido's fault.

Marta and Pina and I worked our fingers to the bone in the kitchen, but still our Christmas feast was a disaster.

First, the apprentices poured cup after cup of rich red wine down their throats, and then Antonio began to flirt with me again. In turn, Piero's face turned to thunder and Pina's face was almost green with jealousy. She spilled wine all down my dress –

on purpose, I'm sure – as she stamped round the table.

"She's wearing the shawl her sweetheart sent her," she hissed in Antonio's ear, loud enough for the whole table to hear.

I pretended I hadn't heard. I didn't want to explain that I had no sweetheart, in case it encouraged Antonio further. But all this nonsense distracted me until I suddenly noticed that Antonio and Piero weren't the only ones who couldn't hold their drink.

"So, you're saying it's all my father's fault?" Guido's voice was raised and his words slurred.

"Not at all," came my father's voice, deeper and lower and with his usual pleasant tone. "It could have happened to whoever took over work on the tower thirty years ago. And your father Giovanni did take steps to correct the tower's tilt."

"But you're saying those steps didn't work – that he didn't have a clue what he was doing!"

Guido was really fired up now, defending his family's honour as fiercely as I would do mine.

"None of us knows exactly what will happen – whatever we do about the leaning tower," my father said. "We have our theories, but the ground shifts in ways we can't predict, and so does the tower itself."

"Yet you think you know better than anyone else," Guido shouted, and he staggered to his feet. He was still holding a cup full of wine and I wished I had noticed sooner what was happening. "Well, here's a challenge to you, Giovanni Pisano!" he yelled. "If you are so much better than my father and me then *you* solve the problem of the tower. If we are all alive in ten years' time, then let us come together again, on Christmas Eve 1308. If you've stopped the tower from tilting – mind, I don't say corrected it, just stopped the angle getting worse – then, then ... then the feast is on me!"

He drained his cup then slammed it down on the table and lurched to the door, where he tried three times to grab the handle. At last he stumbled out into the cold night air, which I hoped would sober him up on the way home.

"I don't know about the tower leaning," Orsello the joiner said. "But I do know Guido can't stand straight!"

Soon everyone was laughing and refilling their glasses, but I could see my father was hurt. He didn't need Guido's challenge to remind him of his duty. It was his job to stop our tower from leaning – indeed from falling right over! A drunken man can lurch and fall and stand up again, but a tower, once it leans beyond a certain angle, will go down for ever.

The party seemed to go on for ever too. I couldn't wait for everyone to go home. It was past midnight by the time the men stumbled off to their beds and my father sent me and Marta and Pina to ours, saying that the clearing up could wait till morning.

And yet he woke me so early that I thought he couldn't have been to bed at all. He put his fingers to his lips.

"Hurry, Netta," he whispered. "Get dressed and come with me."

We slipped out into the chilly air, me wrapping my red shawl tight round me. But we weren't going far – only to the cathedral.

It was too early even for the Mass of the Dawn, but the cathedral door was open, as it always was.

My father walked to a chair near the High Altar and told me to sit down and wait. I didn't know what I was waiting for and I was sleepy. My eyelids closed and the next thing I knew my father was shaking me awake for the second time that morning.

"Look!" he said, and he pointed to the altar. A tall shadow had fallen over it, cast by the weak morning sun rising and shining through the east window. It was like a finger touching the most sacred part of the church.

"The tower!" I gasped, as I recognised its familiar shape. I noticed, too, that now there were other people in the great church with us, transfixed by the magical, holy shadow.

My father nodded. "It was old God Save You's plan," he said softly. "He worked it out so the shadow would fall across the altar on Christmas morning. No one can tell me that such a man didn't know how to design foundations for a tower that would stand for hundreds of years." He sighed. "I would love to design something so glorious."

Father put his arm around me and we watched in silence as the shadow passed and the morning service began. "Happy Christmas," he whispered, and he drew me close.

My heart was light as I went back home to face the mess of last night's feast in the kitchen. Somehow I was sure we would find a way to solve the problem of the tower.

CHAPTER FOURTEEN

A New Year

A week later the first of January dawned, cold and crisp. I couldn't believe there was only one more year to go before the century turned. There was no one alive today who had seen that happen and none of us would ever see it again. The New Year celebrations were always exciting in Pisa, and I could imagine just how big they would be next year.

Even though the official New Year didn't start till the 25th of March, we always had candlelit processions and parties on the 1st of January. And then we did it all again in March. Pisans liked to take every possible opportunity for a party.

"Now you will see why God Save You designed the tower's terraces the way he did!" my father said.

It wasn't the first time I'd seen the tower filled with people, but I had never taken notice the way I did now. They climbed the marble staircase between the two walls and spilled out between the slender columns on to the terraces. Most headed for the second and third floors.

It gave them a wonderful view of the procession, which was winding its way up the Via Santa Maria from the town.

I was up on the fourth floor with my father, where there were fewer people.

"Don't they feel nervous about the tower tilting?" I whispered to him as I looked down and saw all the heads leaning out towards the cathedral.

He gave me a strange look. "Do you?" he asked.

We were on the west side of the tower, as we had been the first time my father had taken me up the marble staircase, and the tilt was to the south.

I could sense it but I felt perfectly safe. I couldn't explain why.

I shook my head. None of the people below and around us felt anything but the wonder of the moment. Not one of us was thinking about the tower falling and flinging us to the ground where we would be crushed by heavy marble stonework.

I smiled at Father and he smiled back. The procession reached the door on the east side of the cathedral. It was named for our Patron Saint, Ranieri, whose tomb is inside the cathedral and covered with images of the life of Christ and His mother.

"Do you see what a good view we have?" my father said. "That's why the tower is built off-centre, so it can overlook the door of the Saint."

The procession filed in until the last candle had disappeared and the piazza seemed pitch-dark by contrast. There was a long, silent pause and then everyone started to descend the tower. We followed them down.

We all filed into the cathedral after the procession and my father and I were with the stragglers at the very end. Just before we went in through Saint Ranieri's door, I turned round to look at the tower.

A full moon lit up the piazza, casting magical shadows around us. Again I had the feeling that the tower would survive and that my father and I would solve the problem of its tilt together. Guido would have to pay for that feast in ten years' time.

The months flew past and we celebrated the New Year all over again in March. A whole year had passed since Measurement Day and there had been no new building work done on the tower.

My father had accepted me as his pupil. And so I learned about precise measurements and angles, about how to calculate weights and tensions – but in secret, as no one knew it except us. Father also had much other work to supervise in the complex of buildings in the piazza and wasn't always with me. At those times he would give me problems to solve and parts of buildings to study.

My head was full of spires and towers, buttresses and columns, and Marta was forever muttering and grumbling about how much time I spent out of the house.

But whenever Father and I had time together, there was only one subject to discuss – our tower and how to fix it.

"There *should* be eight floors," my father said. "That was what God Save You wanted. And the top floor should have the bells, all twelve of them. Think how wonderful it will be to see them all swinging and hear them sounding out their music!"

We were enchanted by this vision, but we always came back to the fact that another floor would add more weight to the tower. And the bells too, cast in metal, would add weight. The tower seemed stable at the moment, but how could we predict what so much extra weight would do to the tilt?

August came and we got ready for the next big procession and feast – the Assumption of the Blessed Virgin Mary. Great dinners would be held in the open air under the stars and there would be the grandest procession yet with hundreds of flickering candles leading from the centre of the town to the cathedral, which was dedicated to Mary of the Assumption.

Again the tower would be full of people watching and again its strength would be tested.

A letter came for my father the day before the procession, which was a rare event in itself. At first he wouldn't tell me what was in it, but he kept looking at me oddly until I got it out of him.

"It is from my friend Tommaso in Siena," he said. "Filippo's father."

"Oh, is he well?" I asked. We both knew who I meant.

"Very well," he said. "In fact, I don't know how to tell you this, but he is getting married tomorrow."

I shouldn't have felt anything at all. But, at my father's words, a pang of sheer shock jolted through my body as if I had been struck by lightning.

CHAPTER FIFTEEN

Solutions

I had no choice but to shake myself and fix my mind on the coming celebrations. I was *not* going to think about what Filippo's wife might be like. I had turned him down and he had every right to make another choice. I told myself this very severely, but found that I had to repeat it to myself more than once.

One thing was certain – the woman he was marrying would not be like me. She would not spend all her waking hours thinking about a tower and how it leaned. She would be content with a handsome, curly-haired husband and her life of babies and chores.

"Is there any way we can make the belfry floor heavier on the north side than on the south?" I asked my father.

It wasn't the first time we had discussed this. But somehow it now seemed urgent. If I'd refused to marry Filippo because I wanted to work on the tower, it was vital that I solve the problem of the eighth floor. I had something to prove to myself.

"Well," he said. "We could build iron weights into the wall on the north side."

"We could," I said. "But there are only two ways, aren't there? Either we make the north side heavier or the south side lighter."

"I have puzzled over it all so long," he said, "that I sometimes doubt I will ever hear the bells ring."

"That's it!" I almost shouted. "Can't we hang the heavier bells on the north side and the lighter ones on the south? Would that make enough difference?"

My father looked stunned. "I don't know," he said. "The design is for six large and six small bells with the large ones hanging underneath the small ones. But we could have the bells cast at any weight we want, provided they ring out the notes of the scale."

We had no time to work out the weights and measurements of the bells just then, but all through the night's celebrations we both thought hard about this solution. My father and I climbed to the seventh floor to watch the procession. We wanted to be at the top, as close as we could be to the missing eighth floor that we longed to build.

The first thing Father said to me next morning was, "I'm not sure adjusting the bells will be enough."

My spirits sank. I'd been so sure I had come up with the solution.

"What else is there?" I asked. I felt that we had been going round and round the same arguments for months, just as if we'd been walking round and round the inside of the tower, on and on for no reason.

"Can we do anything with the steps?" I said, thinking of the staircase again.

"Perhaps," my father said, and his eyes lit up. "Come with me!"

We hurried to his workshop, forgetting all pretence that I wasn't working with him. The apprentices stared with their mouths open as Father riffled through the parchment on his work table, looking for a piece clean enough to use.

He grabbed one and started to scribble lines on it with a stick of charcoal.

"See," he said. "We could have four steps on the north and six on the south and build the south side higher."

He was sketching a circular belfry with elegant arches for bells, such as I had seen him draw before. Other pieces of parchment on his table had sketches of the seven existing floors. But the one he had chosen for the belfry was smaller and showed the work at a lesser scale.

He carried on explaining and drawing until I asked him to stop. I shifted the drawings around until the smaller belfry picture sat on top of a drawing of the tower.

"What are you doing?" he asked.

"Suppose you built the belfry floor smaller than the others," I said, excited. "Then you could rest the outer wall of the belfry on the inner wall of the tower. Wouldn't that make it stronger?"

My father gazed at me in astonishment. Then he let out a yell.

He grabbed me by the hands and we danced round the workshop. The apprentices looked as if we had gone mad. And in a sense we had. After all these months of straining to find an answer to the problems of building the last floor of the tower, we had come up with three in less than a day.

I would never have thought of the last one if I hadn't seen the sheets of parchment all jumbled up. Or if my father had chosen a bigger sheet for his sketch of the belfry.

We stopped our wild dance, out of breath.

"Are you sure this is it?" I asked.

"Quite sure," he said. "We shall do all three things."

"When can we start?"

CHAPTER SIXTEEN

God Save You

From then on we spent every spare moment working out the measurements and design for this smaller, circular belfry we wanted to see on top of our tower. The apprentices got quite used to seeing me walk past their hut to my father's workshop. I had given up all housework now and just ate whatever Marta and Pina put before me. They had to remind me to change my dusty clothes.

I could see the eighth floor in my mind's eye. "It will be like a crown," I said.

It was only a part of a building, but this was the first test of my ability to 'make a building in my mind' that could be turned into a reality.

We had already talked for weeks about the design of the belfry and all we had to do was to scale it down, to carry out my idea of resting its outer wall on the inner wall of the existing tower.

But first we had to build a terrace for it to stand on.

What a thing to be part of!

It was the proudest moment of my life!

Some months later, I was down on the terrace of the seventh floor, looking up at the beginning of the eighth and final floor when a group of masons put the first blocks into place – all of 126 years after the tower's foundations had first been laid.

I had no idea how long the tower would last for, but it had already stood for over a hundred years. I thought again how much more lasting the work of men's hands was than the work of women's bodies. Children made of flesh and bone were so vulnerable, so likely to die at birth or in infancy. And how short those children's lives were even if they reached adulthood. Much shorter than those of buildings, which could survive for hundreds of years.

My own father at close to half a century was nearly an old man.

He was climbing down from the new terrace now and smiled to see me so rapt in my delight that we had started to build again at last.

"You look happy, Netta," he said. "And so you should. It was your idea to make the top floor smaller and now it's going to happen."

He came to sit beside me as we both gazed up past the wooden scaffolding.

"You know what I want next?" I asked.

"Tell me."

"To watch while masons create the first whole building I have designed myself."

"That is a fine ambition," he said. "Though a very unusual one for a woman. I begin to think I have a son after all."

"No, Father, just a daughter who wants to follow in your footsteps. Perhaps I will be given a nickname like God Save You's *Diotisalvi* ..."

"What like 'Let me build'?" he joked. "*Lasciamicostruire?* It would be quite a mouthful."

We both laughed at that.

"How long do you think it will take to finish the terrace?" I asked, still smiling.

"Some months yet," he said. "But it should be in place by the end of the year."

"In time for the new century."

I found this very satisfying. The movement from one century to another seemed so important that it made me believe anything was possible. Like – a woman becoming an architect.

"But I might not be able to supervise the whole of the belfry," my father said. "It could be years yet before the bells can be installed. And, as Head Mason, I am responsible for all the monuments in the piazza. I can't spend all my time on the bell tower, however much I might want to."

"Can your pupils cope on their own?" I asked.

"They needn't be on their own," he said. "You could oversee the work, couldn't you? After me, no one knows the design of the belfry as well as you do."

I couldn't think of anything I would like more, but would the masons listen to a seventeen-year-old female?

My father saw the doubt in my face.

"Don't worry," he said. "I will be close by. We can still do it together. And I'll be around to help at least until the terrace is finished."

My father was right. By the time that 1299 slipped into the new century of 1300, the bell tower had the basis for its final floor – the floor that its first builder, the man nicknamed God Save You, had imagined topping the building at a hundred *braccia*.

In February, Pope Boniface declared 1300 to be a year of "jubilee" – a word I had never heard before. A jubilee meant that everyone was pardoned for their sins, even the dead!

And so, when Guido turned up at our house begging pardon for the scene he had made at our feast the Christmas before last, my father pardoned him … and clasped his hands to declare the scene quite forgotten. (I noted not so kindly that no one had invited Guido to the Christmas feast just gone.)

"But I meant one thing I said," Guido insisted. "I will pay for the Christmas feast just as soon as your belfry is finished and I think that will be long before 1308!"

Two Lives

Pisa, 1316

Well, old Guido was wrong.

I have lived more years since Measurement Day than I had before it and there is a lot to tell about the progress of the tower. And about much else besides.

As he predicted, my father was called away to work on another project, but he didn't have to go far. He was commissioned to build a new pulpit for our cathedral. What an honour!

His father, my grandfather Nicola, had built the pulpit in the Baptistery and both of them had worked on the one in Siena cathedral.

But this was my father's most ambitious work yet, his masterpiece. It was circular in design and raised on sturdy marble pillars that rested on the backs of lions, like the one my grandfather had built in the Baptistery.

It was finished in 1310 and people came from far and wide to see it. I knew he had created a lasting monument to his great skill and artistry.

You see, my beloved father died last year. He was 65 years old and still sculpting. But he didn't die without grandchildren.

How can I explain it? It wasn't what I expected from my life.

In 1303, we had another visit from Filippo. He was now a widower – his wife had died in childbirth in the first year of his marriage, and their baby too. I thought straight away, 'That's what would have happened to me if I'd agreed to marry him.'

His grief had drawn lines into his handsome face that made him look much older. He was very quiet and the only attention he paid me was as the daughter of his father's friend. It was as if he had quite forgotten that he once asked me to marry him.

The men talked about the pulpit and I joined in only when the conversation turned to the belfry, which was progressing slowly.

"Netta has been in charge," my father said.

Filippo looked at me properly for the first time and smiled.

"This was what you wanted to do, wasn't it?" he said. "I'm happy for you."

This time he seemed in no hurry to go back to Siena. As the days passed, we spent a lot of time together in my father's workshop or up on the top of the tower looking out at Pisa. And I got to know Filippo and to see he was a good man with a kind heart.

In fact, I began to think that if only I didn't have to leave Pisa, my father and the tower, I could imagine being happy to marry Filippo.

One day I asked him if he was not needed back at home in Siena.

"Not really," he said. "I have two brothers to help my father in his workshop. And the city feels a sad place to me now."

It was the first time he had referred to his loss.

After another month, I couldn't wait any longer and I asked Filippo to marry me.

I was still afraid of childbirth and I wanted to stay in Pisa but I was 22 now and not the innocent girl I'd been six years before.

I don't know who was the most surprised, Filippo or my father.

But we were married by the end of the year and my new husband was happy to live with us in Pisa. The next year our first son was born. We called him Nicola after my grandfather and he was the apple of my father's eye.

Once I had survived the birth of my first child, Filippo and I went on to have three more sturdy boys, Tommaso, Giovanni and Filippino. Three years later I had twin daughters – Francesca, after my mother, and Simonetta after me. Motherhood no longer filled me with fear.

That was the year before my father died. So he was blessed with four grandsons and two grand-daughters.

Just before he died, Father said, "I want you to teach them all about building and stone-carving, Netta. Not just the boys. Find which of your children take after you and me and train them, inspire them to follow us."

"You forget their father shares our craft," I said, and I smoothed back his sparse white hair. "If we are lucky, they will *all* take after us."

Filippo worked alongside my father until his death and is now one of his best-known pupils. He has been looking after the tower too, and so have I whenever I could get away from the care of my children.

Old Marta died soon after little Nicola was born and Pina is long gone, married to Antonio, who is now a proper stone-carver and mason. Success came his way, after all! So we have two new women to run the house and look after us and a nurse for the younger children. My little girls are old enough to leave in someone else's care and I still climb the tower when I can.

I can see for miles from the top, but not as far as I would like.

I want to see into the future, a future where my girls could work alongside their brothers and their father – and me.

I still want to design a building in my mind and see it grow out of the ground from strong foundations to stand tall and – I hope – straight.

I know now that I can live two lives at once – a mother to my six children and an architect and builder like my father and my husband. Perhaps we'll have to pretend that the designs are Filippo's until the rest of the world has caught up with the year 1316.

But I'm sure we will get there in the end, just as I am sure that the leaning tower of Pisa will continue to stand.

About *Tilt*

Giovanni Pisano is a real person (1250 – c.1315), who worked as Head Mason in Pisa and was the most likely person to have begun building the eighth floor of its famous tower. His father was Nicola Pisano, but I could find out nothing about any family members who came after him, so Netta, Filippo and their six children are all invented.

The (Leaning) Tower of Pisa took two hundred years to build, but not continuously, as its foundations were laid in 1173 and its bells not added to the eighth-floor belfry till 1373.

It is unlikely that the Netta of my invention was alive to see that great moment.

Mary Hoffman

MARY HOFFMAN is famous for her brilliant, vivid novels in which fictional characters bring history to life.

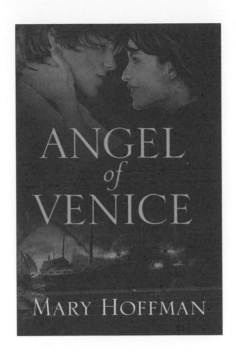

Venice, 1571

In the great shipyard of the Arsenale, Luca fetches water, chops wood and lights fires. As he works, he dreams of a girl with hair as gold as an angel's and skin as soft as a white peach.

But Venice is preparing for war – war against the mighty Ottoman Empire. And so Luca boards *The Angel* and sets sail.

Life at sea is thrilling, but Luca will need his wits about him to survive the terrible battle that lies ahead …

Our books are tested
for children and young people by
children and young people.

Thanks to everyone who consulted on
a manuscript for their time and effort in
helping us to make our books better
for our readers.